ST. NICH AND THE DOGS OF ROME

Russell Claxton

Blue Igloo Books

For all the dogs who've ever been without a home.

Copyright 2015
Russell Claxton

All rights reserved. Published by Blue Igloo Books.
Blue Igloo Books and associated logos are trademarks and/or registered trademarks of Blue Igloo Books.
www.blueigloobooks.com

No part of this publication may be reproduced, stored in digital format for retrieval or transmitted in any form or by any means without written permission from Blue Igloo Books.

Library of Congress Control Number: 2015917387

Summary: Sally, heroine of the earlier book, The St. Nicholas Yorkies, is going to college in Rome, where she immediately sets about continuing a commitment to the rescue of stray dogs. St. Nick and his wife Zoe, who've never forgotten how she saved Christmas eight years ago, do all they can to help.

ISBN 978-0-9884828-5-2
[Juvenile Fiction / Holidays & Celebrations / Christmas & Advent / Stories in Verse]

10 9 8 7 6 5 4 3 2 1
First Edition

Prologue

On Christmas Eve, 1946, St. Nicholas with his team of Elves and reindeer had to crash land into York, England. The reindeer had fallen sick and weren't able to continue. Nicholas was at a loss as to what to do. A young girl suddenly appeared with her puppy and offered to round up enough Yorkshire Terriers to pull the sleigh. Lacking a better alternative, he agreed.

The girl, Sally, and her Yorkie, Bitsy, quickly recruited 44 Yorkies, and they were able to save Christmas from being the first in many, many years without presents for all the world's children.

St. Nicholas never forgot this. He and his wife, Zoe, stayed in touch with Sally and her family, and Nick made a custom of York being the last stop on Christmas morning, having breakfast with them to catch up on the year's events.

Eight years after the Yorkie Christmas, Sally is ready to go to college, and has won a scholarship to study in Rome. St. Nicholas arranged for Zoe to spend Christmas Eve night with Sally's family, and joined them for breakfast Christmas morning.

York.
Christmas Eve, 1946

York.
Christmas Morning, 1954

"The scholarship seemed a long shot,
A story with unlikely plot.
To live there while in college seems
To be more than I'd ever dream."

Airport, Rome, Italy.

"Tomorrow, breakfast once again,
Villa Armento, with our friends.
Your mom and I spoke with them both,
And they would love to be your hosts."

"Signora, Rome's a charming place
With marks of time upon its face.
Some parts are vast and some are small,
But, I'm quite sure you'll like them all!"

"Something you'll sense when you are there,
Is ancient hist-ry everywhere.
Its traces cling to all the stones,
Though most the names are now unknown."

Villa Armento
Palatine Hill, Rome
Home of Anthony and Cosima Armento

"Old and storied, there's just one Rome,
It's the place where all roads lead home."
"Tomorrow, Sally, we'll go see
A friend who rescues cats. Agree?"

"One thing I've learned from tending cats,
You meet the costs, or it falls flat.
Food, the medicines, and the vets,
And there is more - that you can bet!
A benefit, a masquerade,
If done just right, we'll have it made!"

"Now, Zoe, you and Nick must come.
We need a 'draw' to beat the drum!
This pays for cats and pays for dogs,
See! All of Rome will be agog!"

Old Capitol of Rome, The Campodoglio

Capitoline Hill, citadel of the earliest Romans.
Statue of Marcus Aurelius, Emperor 161-180 A.D., at
the center of the Piazza. Buildings and Piazza in their
present form designed by Michaelangelo in 1536-1546.

"A story - the statue up ahead,
For many long years it was said,
Was of Emperor Constantine,
First Christian ruler on the scene.
Finally, they grew suspicious -
This statue's Marcus Aurelius!"

"Pagan statues were melted down
For new ones when rulers were crowned.
Pagan was Marcus Aurelius
But fate is sometimes capricious.
This mistake was the only way
Marcus Aurelius is here today!"

Palazzo Nuovo

Palazzo Senatorio

Palazzo dei Conservatori

Capitoline Wolf
Palazzo dei Conservatori

"Romulus and Remus, the founders of Rome,
Nurtured by a she-wolf, and this was their home.
From small, little infants, to great and strong men,
The city grew great, too, but so tiny then.
Somewhere on the streets here, who knows? Could be true,
The she-wolf's descendents, are in need of you."

"Do you like dogs? I thought you might!
I rescue strays - it's a delight!
I need a little help from friends,
Mostly to get the dogs in pens.

"Rome seems to have a lot of strays,
You see them everywhere these days.
Just think, most never had a home,
Or friendly word, so they just roam."

"You see, we've planned a big event,
And we just got city's assent
To use the old Colosseo
For a great big 'adopteo!'"

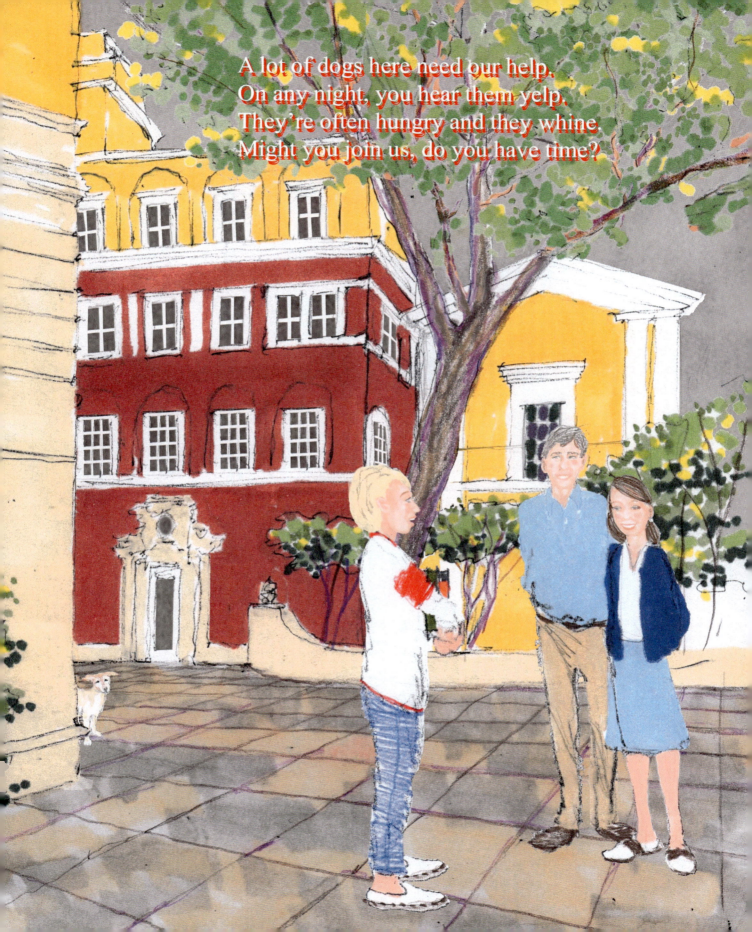

A lot of dogs here need our help.
On any night, you hear them yelp.
They're often hungry and they whine.
Might you join us, do you have time?

Dear Sally,

I spoke with Raspinel, and would like him to come with me to visit you in Rome. We can introduce you to a friend, who can help insure that you are safe while you go about your work in the rescue of dogs in Rome.

Our friend is a gypsy king, named Scaramuccia. We call him Scara for short. Don't worry, there is nothing scary about him. He is Raspinel's good friend and will make sure that you and your dogs are safe in the City of Seven Hills.

We will call you when we arrive.

Ciao, Nicholas

Casa Rodi

"This is where we'll camp this year
If you can see the coast is clear,
Police won't come here in the night,
And run us off, I fear they might."

"Don't worry Scara, there'll be peace
Between your clan and the police.
The Police Chief, too, wants good homes
For all these stray dogs loose in Rome"

Trajan's Market and Casa dei Cavalieri di Rodi

Trajan's Market was likely the world's first shopping mall. Built by Emperor Trajan just after 100 A.D., it held administrative offices in addition to shops and vendor stalls. Free grain was distributed for many years.
Casa dei Cavalieri di Rodi (House of the Knights of Rhodes) was built after 1,200 A.D. adjacent to the site of Trajan's Market, above the ruins of the Forum of Augusta. Since 1946, it has belonged to the Sovereign Order of Malta, the oldest surviving order of chivalry.

"This view is grand, you see so far,
The history, of peace and war.
The Roman Forum, there it lies,
Beneath the brightest Roman sky.

"That's where the strays are, Sally, dear.
Nights it's empty - they have less fear."

"The sun's been down for just two hours,
Here's two strays - yes, neither is ours.

"This music is so wonderful.
It's so delicate but soulful.
It's soothing but it stimulates
So, where did it originate?"

"Our music comes from India,
The same as Romani people.
It quickly spread to Southern Spain
Flamenco ought to have our name."

Fancy chickens catch the eye,
Polish hens don't like to fly.
If they're riled up, though, you'd best run.
Those roosters fight you, just for fun!

"These chickens can't be very tough.
We'll scare them if we're bold enough."

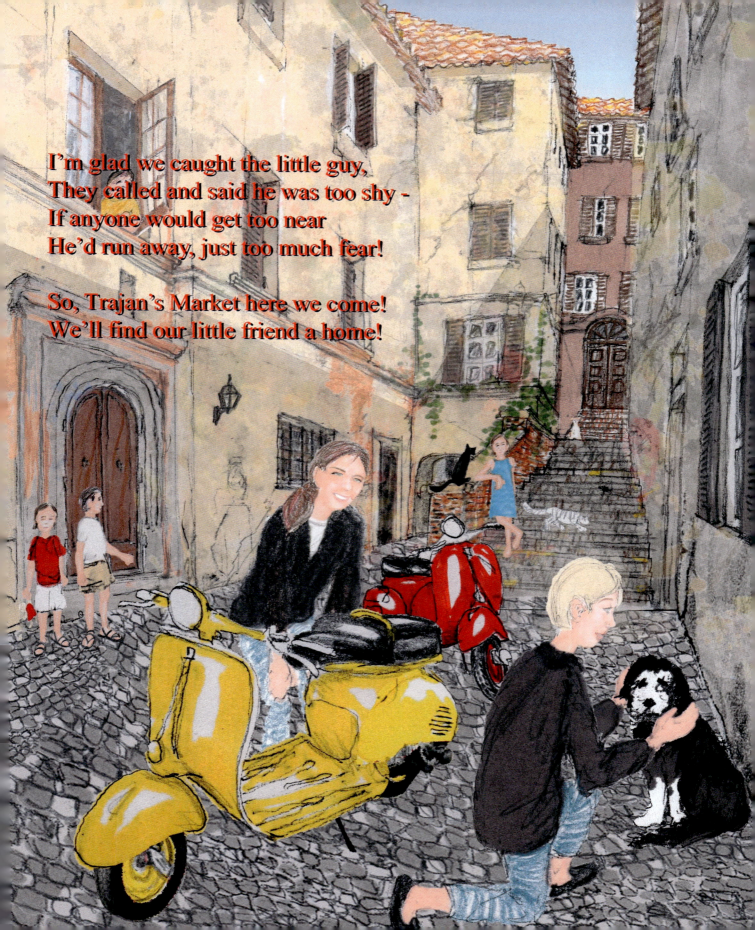

St. Peter's Square

Designed by Gian Lorenzo Bernini from 1656 to 1667, the square is adjacent to St. Peter's Basilica, 1506 to 1626, and lies to its east. The ancient Egyptian obelisk at its center was brought to Rome in 37 A.D., placed in its present location in 1586. Bernini's colonnade, shaped as an ellipse and a trapezoid, is four columns deep, making a large space for gatherings, 320 x 240 meters.

"A pretty dog, what kind is he?"
"A Yorkie handful, as you see!"

Piazza Navona

Neptune's Fountain
Built 1574, Sculptures added 1873
Neptune was the Roman god of the seas and earthquakes.
His importance owed to Italy's being surrounded by water,
and his temperamental earthquakes.

"Is that your dog?" "No, sir, it's not.
He's often here in this same spot.
He's sometimes near Colosseo,
He's little, and called Piccolo!
We try to catch him, runs away.
He needs a home where he can stay."

Ostia Antica Ruins
Ancient Roman Mediterranian port city, 20 miles from Colosseum.

Trajan's Market

Now, Rome's a very pretty place
Where dogs are fun to spot and chase.
But, in the end, like everywhere,
The thing's to bring them needed care.

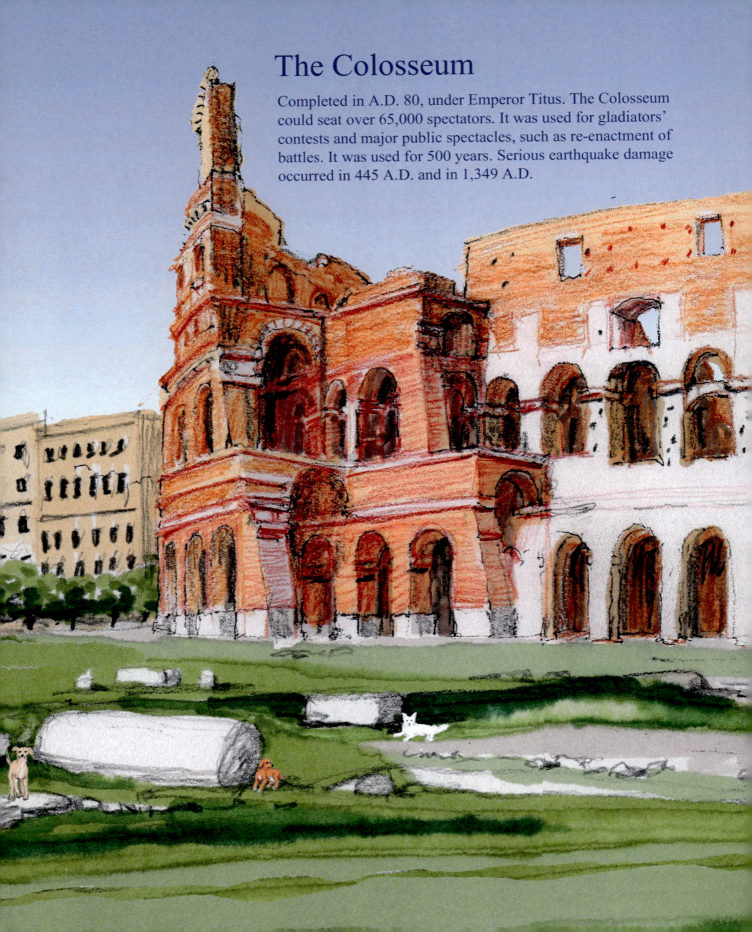

The Colosseum

Completed in A.D. 80, under Emperor Titus. The Colosseum could seat over 65,000 spectators. It was used for gladiators' contests and major public spectacles, such as re-enactment of battles. It was used for 500 years. Serious earthquake damage occurred in 445 A.D. and in 1,349 A.D.

"This has to be the one, best place.
Adoptions need a lot of space
To herd the dogs and park the cars
It can't be crowded like bazaars!"

"Tomorrow morning - I can't wait!
The turnout's going to be great!
Posters hung in churches and schools,
Movies, cafes - this is so cool!

"We'll get here, set up at sunrise.
Give me a hand, let's get these guys."

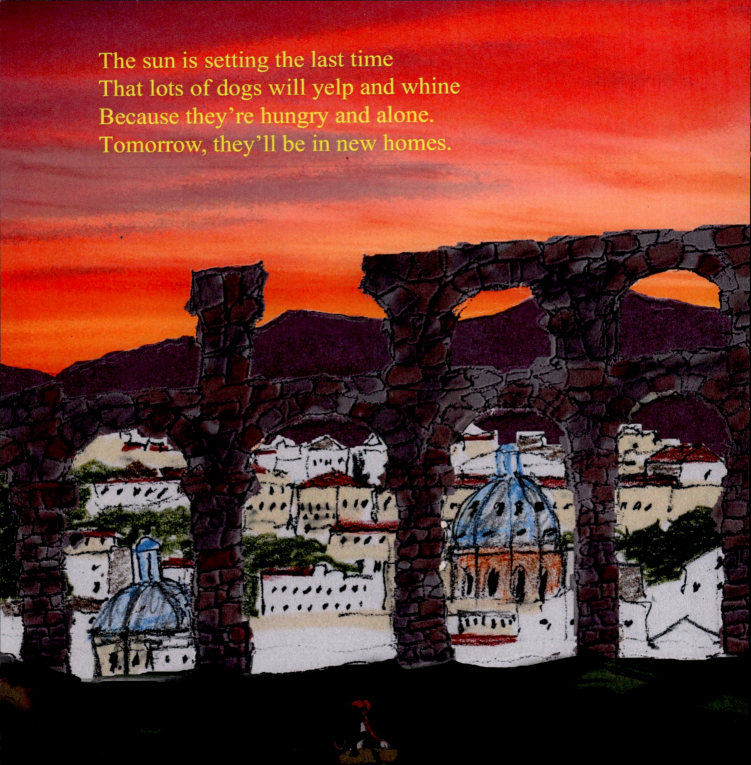

"So, both your lives forever changed!
And, you said Beanie's now his name?
He'll have full tummy and soft bed,
He'll wag his tail, you'll pat his head.
He'll wait for you when you're away -
When you come home, you've made his day."

ADDOTARE UN CANE

"Ma'am, so many dogs! How to choose?"
"If that tail wags, you just can't lose!"

"So, this is little Piccolo!
He's going with you to Tromso!"
"I have a cat who stowed away
One Christmas Eve inside the sleigh.
He chose me, I suppose we'd say,
But, Piccolo always ran away!"

The passers-by all heard a cheer.
The funds were raised - for a whole year.
For lots of dogs out on the streets,
With little food, and never treats.

She saved Christmas in Forty-Six.
He never thought she'd top that trick.

Nick quite nearly shed a tear.
This kid had saved another year -
This time for strays - they'd now have homes,
Next Christmas Day, these dogs of Rome.

THE BOOK'S SCENE LOCATIONS IN ROME

This is a small part of Rome. Some scenes are futher away and aren't shown.

Also by Russell Claxton

THE ST. NICHOLAS YORKIES
SAVING CHRISTMAS DAY

A Christmas tale of near-disaster, and a spirited response from the people and dogs of York.

The story will probably delight anyone who's ever known a dog.

Or a reindeer.

Or a cat.

ST. NICHOLAS AND FRIENDS
THE WHOLE YEAR ROUND

Come along for the ride! See how St. Nicholas and friends spend the year of 1947 having fun and getting ready for the long night's work on Christmas Eve.

ST. NICHOLAS IN PARIS
PRESIDENTS, POODLES, AND PARADES

1959. An invitation from the president of France brings St. Nick and the whole team to Paris for a visit, the Carnival, and a state dinner in appreciation for his work.

There were some surprises, too.

THE ST. NICHOLAS OWLS
AND THE LUCKIEST LAB

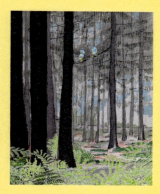

From a pair of unearthly eggs to a sharp-eyed rescue, the owls bring a new dimension to the St. Nicholas team in Tromso, and a new Labrador puppy.

www.blueigloobooks.com

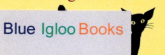

About the author

Russell Claxton, a Texas native, has called Macon, Georgia home for over twenty-five years with his wife Natalie and a string of dogs, cats and wildlife.

He is a practicing architect and urban designer. The conservation of natural resources runs high on his list of priorities.

Animal well-being is a life-long preoccupation, with accompanying enjoyment and appreciation of dogs, cats and lots of other animal friends.

Made in the USA
Columbia, SC
14 August 2022